Postman Pat

ANNUAL 2001

Illustrated by Baz Rowell

Charlie Chalk illustrated by Ray Mutimer

Written by Brenda Apsley

Designed by Julie Clough

POSTMAN PAT © Woodland Animations Limited 2000.
Licensed by Copyrights. The Post Office's imagery
reproduced under licence. All rights reserved.
Published in Great Britain by Egmont World Limited,
a division of Egmont Holding Limited.
Egmont World Limited, Deanway Technology Centre,
Wilmslow Road, Handforth, Cheshire SK9 3FB.
Printed in Italy.
ISBN 0 7498 4863 4

£5.99
UK only

CW00358307

Contents

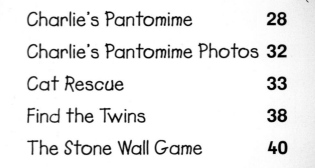

Birdwatching

One day, Julian was watching the birds in the garden. He was looking in a book of bird pictures to find their names.

"There are lots of birds in the garden," said Postman Pat. "But you can see more out in the woods. Let's do some birdwatching on Sunday."

"That's a great idea, Dad!" said Julian. "I'll take my bird book with me."

On Sunday, Pat and Julian got up very early. It was still dark. "I'll sort out what we need to take with us," said Pat. "We want to see the birds, but we don't want them to see us. We'll watch them in disguise."

"How can we do that?" asked Julian.

"We'll wear clothes that match the colours of the things around us, like trees and leaves. Animals and birds use colour as a disguise, too. It's called camouflage."

5

Julian watched as Pat packed an old tent into his rucksack. "Are we staying out all night, Dad?" he asked.

"No," said Pat. "We're going to use the tent as a sort of shelter. It's green, so the birds won't notice it, and we can hide under it. Birdwatchers call something like this a hide, and that's what we're going to do with it – hide from the birds!"

Pat packed two fold-up camping chairs, then he put a pair of binoculars around Julian's neck. "When you look at the birds through these, they'll look as if they are much closer than they really are," Pat told him.

"There's just one more thing," said Pat. He showed Julian some big fancy feathers. "Granny Dryden gave me these. She took them off an old hat she was throwing away." Pat stuck some of the feathers into Julian's woolly hat, and some into his own. "Perfect camouflage!"

Pat and Julian walked to the edge of the woods. "We'll make our hide behind that hedge," said Pat. "It's a good place to wait and watch. If we're quiet, the birds won't notice us."

Pat was right. He and Julian saw lots of birds. Julian drew pictures of some of them.

"You don't have to see birds to know they are around," said Pat. "Listen! Can you hear that whistling song? It's a blackbird. And that soft coo-coo sound is a wood pigeon."

Just then, Julian heard a different sort of noise. CLICK! CLICK! CLICK! it went. "Is it a woodpecker, Dad?" whispered Julian.

Pat looked puzzled and shook his head. "No," he said.

They heard the noise again. CLICK! CLICK! CLICK!

"I don't know which bird makes a noise like that," said Pat.

When Pat and Julian got home, Sara told them about a talk at the village hall. "Major Forbes is showing his photographs of Greendale birds," she said. "You should go."

Pat and Julian enjoyed the Major's talk. At the end, he pinned up some extra-large photographs. "I've kept my best photographs till last because they are so unusual," he said. "This amazing bird is one I have never seen before, even in a book. Look at these big, bright feathers! This must be a very rare bird indeed."

Julian giggled, and nudged Pat, who had a big smile on his face.

"Look, Dad," said Julian. "Those feathers are the ones you stuck in your woolly hat! Major Forbes didn't take those photographs of a bird. He took them of you! That clicking sound we heard was his camera!"

Pat nodded. "Yes," he said. "The Major has taken some photographs of a very rare bird indeed – the postman bird!"

Who's Hiding?

Pat and Julian used camouflage to hide from the birds. It's a sort of disguise. Animals use camouflage to hide from enemies. They match the colours around them, and stay very, very still!

Count the numbers of different animals you can see.
Look carefully – remember, they're hiding!

 sparrows   butterflies

 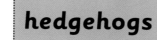 hedgehogs  rabbits

Pat's Birthday Present

1. It is Pat's birthday. His best present is from Sara and Julian – a tiny cassette player with earphones.

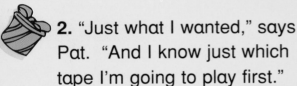

2. "Just what I wanted," says Pat. "And I know just which tape I'm going to play first."

3. Next morning, Pat delivers the post. But he does some very odd things!

4. "What's wrong with Pat?" asks Mrs Goggins. "He's walking round and round the postbox!"

5. Pat walks in front of Miss Hubbard's bike. "Look out, Pat!" she shouts, but he doesn't hear.

6. Granny Dryden watches as Pat claps his hands in the air. "How odd!" she says.

7. PC Selby stops outside Sam's mobile shop. "What's wrong with Pat today?" he asks.

8. "I don't know," says Sam. "I asked, but he just went off down the lane, dancing!"

9. Even Jess the cat is puzzled. He has never seen Pat doing things like this before.

10. Pat doesn't seem to notice people staring and pointing at him. He ignores them.

11. When Pat gets home he gets changed and goes outside to work in the garden.

12. Sara watches Pat from the window. He steps in and out of the carrots in his wellingtons!

13. She goes outside. "What are you doing, Pat?" she asks. But he doesn't answer.

14. Just then, Julian comes home. He smiles when Pat dances around the vegetable patch.

15. Julian reaches into Pat's top pocket. Then he pulls something out of Pat's ears!

16. Pat stands still for the first time that day. "Hey, what are you doing, Julian?" he asks.

17. Sara is very puzzled. So is Jess. "What is going on, you two?" Sara asks.

18. "Dad's wearing his cassette player," says Julian. "I turned it off and took out his earplugs."

19. "So that's why you didn't hear me!" says Sara. "But why were you dancing around like that?"

20. Pat shows Sara a tape. "I was listening to my line dancing tape, and trying some new steps!"

The Paperchase Game

Postman Pat has made a paperchase race.
The children find the pieces of paper Pat has left to follow his trail.

Play the game with a friend.
You need a die and a counter or button each.
Start at I and take turns to roll the die.
Move from paper to paper. If you roll 3, move 3 spaces, and so on.
The first player to reach Postman Pat is the winner.

Pat's Long Walk

Postman Pat was helping out at the bring-and-buy sale in the village hall. "Just look at these old chairs, Pat!" said the Reverend Timms. "The legs are all wobbly. They're falling to bits."

Mrs Goggins had had a busy time selling cakes. "My poor feet are aching," she said. "Pass me a chair, please, Pat, and I'll have a sit-down."

But as Mrs Goggins sat on the chair there was a loud SNAP! and one of the legs fell off. Pat and the Vicar just managed to catch Mrs Goggins before she fell.

"That does it," said the Reverend Timms. "These old chairs have got to

20 go. We'll have to get some money to buy new ones. Any ideas, Pat?"

Pat thought hard for a minute. "What about a country walk?" he said. "We'll ask people to sponsor us, to give us some money if we finish the walk."

"That's a really good idea, Pat," said the Vicar.

Pat had another idea. "Each person who does the walk can try to collect enough money to buy one chair," he said. "If lots of people do the walk, we'll be able to buy lots of new chairs to replace the old ones. And I'll sort out the walk for you. I like walking."

The Reverend Timms laughed. "Yes," he said. "Postmen do know a lot about walking, don't they?"

Pat planned the walk carefully. He looked at his maps to decide where the walk would be.

On his day off Pat walked along the route he had chosen. It went through the village, up into the hills and back along the river.

Then Pat did the walk all over again. Julian went with him. This time he put lots of little sticks on walls and in the ground. "The sticks are markers so the people on the walk will know which way to go," he told Julian. "I don't want anyone getting lost!"

It was late when Pat got home, and his feet were sore. But there was no time for a rest. "I'm going into the village to collect the names of people who are going to sponsor me on the walk tomorrow," he told Sara.

Pat's walk was a great success. Lots of his friends and neighbours took part. The ones who didn't do the walk waited at the church. They cheered and clapped as the walkers came back one by one.

Pat was the first to finish the walk, but he still had work to do. He ticked off the names of the other walkers as they got back, to make sure no one had got lost.

"The last walker has arrived safely now," the Reverend Timms said later. "You can have a rest now, Pat."

But Pat shook his head. "No, I can't," he said. "I've got one more thing to do. I'm going to do the walk one more time, to collect all my little markers. I don't want to leave any litter. See you later."

Pat had to be up early the next day to deliver the post. But there was still no time to rest. "I have to collect the money from my sponsors," he told Sara after he got back from work.

Mrs Goggins was last on Pat's list. "You look tired, Pat," she said. "Go home and have a rest."

"I will," said Pat, "as soon as I've taken the money to the

 24 Reverend Timms."

There was a big van outside the village hall. "Look, Pat," said the Reverend Timms. "The new chairs have arrived. We can throw all the old ones away."

The Reverend Timms looked at the money Pat had collected. "Well done, Pat!" he said. "There's more than enough to pay for a chair here!"

Pat smiled, and sat down on one of the new chairs. "Good," he said. "I really need a sit-down after all the walking I've done!"

Read with Postman Pat

Read this story with Postman Pat. The little pictures will help you.

"It's Pancake Day," says  .

"Let's make one big  for all the

 to share.

Pat makes a  of things he needs:

• *eggs* • *flour* • *milk* •

 gives Pat some

his  have laid. Pat gets some

 of flour from Sam's  .

 gives Pat lots of  from

the  on his .

"I've got a big from to cook

the pancake in," says Pat. "But what can I

mix the and and in?

's isn't big enough."

has just the thing. He shows

Pat his brand new . "I haven't

used it yet," he says.

"It's perfect for my giant !"

laughs .

Charlie's Pantomime

1. "I'm bored!" says Arnold the big pink elephant. "There's nothing to do on Merrytwit!"

2. "So am I!" says Lewis T. Duck. "I wish we could watch something exciting, like a play or a show."

3. "We could put on our own show," says Charlie Chalk. "But what kind? Singing? Dancing?

4. "Both!" says Trader Jones. "Let's do a pantomime. A show like Aladdin or Cinderella."

5. "That's a great idea, Trader!" says Charlie. "And I know just the person to do it – ME!"

6. "I like the idea," says Captain Mildred. "Because a, I love panto and b, I want to be in it!"

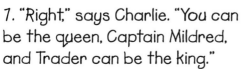

7. "Right," says Charlie. "You can be the queen, Captain Mildred, and Trader can be the king."

8. Arnold is very, very pleased when Charlie says he can play the part of the handsome prince.

9. "Lewis T. Duck can do the music," says Charlie. "And I'm going to be the bad villain!"

10. There's only one person who can fly, so Mary the Hover Fairy will play the part of the good fairy.

11. Everyone wants to be in Charlie's pantomime. They can't wait to get started.

12. Charlie writes the words and songs for the pantomime on paper, and gives them out.

13. "Do you like them?" Charlie asks Mary. "Yes," she says, "but ..." And she points to a coconut tree.

14. Edward is lying flat on his back under the tree. He's fast asleep, as usual, and snoring quietly.

15. "What about Edward?" says Mary. "Did you forget him? He's the only one who isn't in the panto."

16. "Oh yes, he is," says Charlie. "Edward is the star of the show. It's perfect for him – Sleeping Beauty!"

Charlie's Pantomime Photos

Charlie Chalk took his camera to the pantomime.
These are two of the photos he took.

If you look carefully you will see that some things have changed in the bottom picture.
Can you spot 5 differences?

732

Answers: Lewis's trumpet is bigger; Edward's shoes are shiny; Arnold's trousers are a different colour; the bedknobs are square; the curtains are different.

Cat Rescue

One morning, Postman Pat was delivering the post using his little mail trolley. It was nearly empty when he got to Granny Dryden's house, the last one on his round.

Pat looked at his watch. "I'm early today," he said, as he knocked on the door. "I'll have a cup of tea with Granny Dryden before I go back to the Post Office."

But Granny Dryden was too worried to make tea. "I've lost my little cat, Blossom," she said. "I haven't seen her since yesterday. I can't find her anywhere."

"Don't worry," said Pat. "She'll turn up. I bet she's in the garden. I'll go and look."

But Pat could not find Blossom. "I've got to get back to the Post Office now," he told Granny Dryden. "But I'll keep a lookout for her."

As Pat walked towards the church he saw some people standing under one of the tall trees. "Morning!" said Pat. "What's going on?"

PC Selby, the village policeman, pointed up into one of the trees. "There's a cat stuck up the tree," he said. "It's been there all night."

Pat looked up into the tree. He could just see a little ginger cat. "I think it's Granny Dryden's cat, Blossom," said Pat. "I've been looking for her."

Just then, Ted Glen arrived in his van. "Is there anything wrong?" he asked.

PC Selby told Ted that they wanted to get Blossom out of the tree.

"I've got just what you need," said Ted, and he opened the doors of his van. "You can borrow my long ladder to climb up the tree."

Ted held the ladder against the tree so it wouldn't slip, and PC Selby climbed up to the top.

"Can you reach her?" called Pat.

"Yes, but she's very frightened," said PC Selby. "She won't let me get hold of her. I need something to put her in."

"We need a sack, or a box or something," said Ted. "But I haven't got anything like that."

"But I have!" said Pat, and he pointed to his mail trolley.

"Just what we need, Pat!" said Ted. "If you stand on the bottom rungs of the ladder, you can pass the bag up to PC Selby."

PC Selby held the bag by the handle and put it over Blossom. He was very gentle, and got her inside it. "The cat's in the bag now," he said. "Take it from me, will you, Pat? I'll hold on to the handle so it doesn't fall."

Blossom the cat, Pat's bag and PC Selby were soon down on the ground again, safe and sound. "Thanks, Ted. Thanks, Pat," said PC Selby. "I couldn't have rescued the cat without you."

"Granny Dryden will be pleased to have Blossom back," said Pat.

"Yes," said PC Selby. "I'll get the cat out of your bag, Pat, and take her home."

But Pat stopped him. "No, leave her in there," he said. "I'll take her home to Granny Dryden in my bag."

Postman Pat set off to walk back to Granny Dryden's house, pulling his mail trolley. Blossom the cat sat peeping out of the top. She looked as if she was enjoying her ride.

Jess walked behind them. He looked at the mailbag on wheels, and he looked at Blossom having a lift home. Then he looked at Postman Pat as if to say, "**That's** a good idea. A **very** good idea. Now why didn't I think of it?"

Find the Twins

Tom and Katy Pottage are twins. They are the same age, and they look alike. Tom and Katy were very pleased when their pet cat had kittens. They were even more pleased when their mum told them that two of the kittens were twins, just like them.

Can you find the two kittens that are exactly the same?

The Stone Wall Game

Jess the cat loves to sit on top of the stone walls in Greendale.

Play the stone wall game with a friend.
You need a die, and a counter or button each.

Start at stone number 1 and take turns to roll the die.
If you roll 2, move 2 stones. If you roll 3, move 3, and so on.

If you land on move **UP** to the .

If you land on move **DOWN** to the .

If you land on have an extra turn.

If you land on miss a turn.

The first player to climb to the
top of the wall is the winner.

25

18   19

10   11   12

1   2   3   4

Pat Gets Busy

1. The Greendale village hall is a very busy place. There is keep fit, and a line dancing class.

2. One day, Pat meets the Reverend Timms at the hall. "I've got a problem," the Vicar tells him.

3. "Mrs Pottage wants to use the village hall as a meeting place for the children's playgroup."

4. "But why is that a problem?" asks Pat. "It'll be lovely to have lots of children in the hall."

5. "Yes," says the Vicar. "But it's so dark and dull. Children need a bright, cheerful place to play."

6. "I see what you mean," says Pat. "What we need is paint, and lots and lots of it. Leave it to me, Vicar!"

7. Pat gets busy. First, he asks all the people in the village to give him their old tins of paint.

8. Next, he finds lots of people to help him. They meet at the village hall on Saturday morning.

9. "We're going to paint the whole hall," says Pat. "So it looks really special for the children ..."

10. Pat tells them what he wants them to do, and they all get busy. Miss Hubbard uses brown paint.

11. Major Forbes has a big pot of yellow paint. He gets it all over his white moustache!

12. Pat uses lots of bright colours. He wears an old shirt to keep himself clean, but he gets the shirt covered in paint!

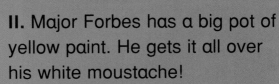

13. Jess wants to help with the painting, too. He uses his paws instead of a paintbrush!

14. Painting the hall is hard work. At last it is finished. "Well done, everyone!" says Pat. "Thanks."

15. Mrs Pottage can't wait to see the hall. She asks the helpers to the first playgroup meeting.

16. The hall is dark when they go in, then Pat turns on the lights. "Welcome to the playgroup!"

Look! Pat and his friends have painted nursery rhyme pictures.

Do you know their names?

Read with Postman Pat

Read this story with Postman Pat. The little pictures will help you.

Sara is hanging out  and

and  on the  .

Julian helps her. He puts  on

the pairs of  .

"I'm going to climb up the

to pick the  ," says Pat.

He goes into the  .

But the  is broken,

and the big  has a hole in it.

"I can't pick the apples now," says  .

 jumps up into the tree.

He walks along the  and

knocks down the apples.

Pat catches them.  helps.

She puts the  in the big

plastic washing basket!

 helps, too. "You can keep

the apples in the  my

 came in!" he says.

Get Well Soon, Pat!

Poor Postman Pat! He had a very bad cold. He was coughing and sneezing, and his nose was red and sore. He couldn't go to work, and had to stay in bed for a whole week.

Everyone who lives in Greendale knows Pat, and they missed seeing him around the village. They liked to say hello when he delivered their letters and parcels.

Pat's friends called Sara on the telephone when they heard he was ill. They sent lots of Get Well Soon cards. Sara put them on the little table at the side of Pat's bed, but there were so many that she had to take some of them downstairs and put them on the mantelpiece.

The Reverend Timms called on Monday. "How is Pat?" he asked.

"He's feeling quite ill," said Sara.

When Mrs Goggins called on Tuesday, Sara told her that Pat was still not well.

Sara told Mrs Pottage the same thing on Wednesday.

On Thursday Sara had better news for Miss Hubbard. "Pat's stopped sneezing now," she said.

Granny Dryden called on Friday.

"Pat is feeling a bit better," Sara told her.

"I feel a lot better today," Pat said when he woke up on Saturday morning. "Pat is feeling much better now," Sara told Peter Fogg.

On Sunday morning, Pat was feeling so much better that he got up, and sat by the fire in his pyjamas and dressing gown.

Sara had good news when Sam Waldron rang to ask how Pat was. "Pat's feeling fine," she told him.

When they heard that Pat was up and about, his friends all came to see him. "I'm glad you're feeling better," said Mrs Goggins. "I've brought you one of my chocolate cakes you like so much."

Granny Dryden came with a big bag of home-made treacle toffee.

Miss Hubbard had baked a big apple pie. "It's still warm from the oven," she said.

Soon the house was full of people and the things they had brought for Pat to eat. There was a basket of eggs from the Thompsons, and a big cheese that Peter Fogg had made from milk from his cows. There was a jar of honey from Major Forbes's bees, and two pots of Mrs Pottage's strawberry jam. The Reverend Timms sent some biscuits, and Doctor Gilbertson called in with a big bottle of rosehip drink.

"Try a little piece of cheese on a cracker," said Peter.

"And some of my strawberry jam," said Mrs Pottage. "Katy made some scones to go with it."

"A slice of my chocolate cake will make you feel better," said Mrs Goggins.

"And you can stir some of my honey into your tea," said Major Forbes.

Pat wasn't very hungry, but he didn't want to hurt their feelings, so he tried a little bit of everything. Even the sticky chocolate truffles Tom Pottage had made. Later, when everyone had gone home, Julian came back from football. "How are you feeling, Dad?" he asked.

Pat patted his tummy, then pointed to the food that was piled up on the table. "Well, Julian," he said, "I **was** feeling a lot better. But eating all this food has made me feel quite poorly again. I think I'll go back to bed!"

Pat's Card Puzzle

Pat got lots of Get Well Soon cards when he was ill. Which of his friends sent which card? Can you match the friends with the cards?

a

b

c

d

e

Tick, Tock!

1. Charlie and his friends are going for a trip on the Buttercup, Captain Mildred's boat.

2. "Now don't be late," says Captain Mildred. "When I ring Buttercup's big bell, I'm off. I won't wait for you."

3. "She means it, Charlie," says Edward, who is always sleepy. "How will we get up on time?"

4. "We'll sleep at my store," says Trader Jones. "I've got a VERY loud alarm clock."

5. That night, Charlie and the others go to sleep. TICK, TOCK! goes the big clock, TICK, TOCK!

6. But Arnold is worried about being late. He turns the clock back so it will wake them up earlier.

7. Arnold creeps back to bed. The others are asleep. TICK TOCK! goes the clock, TICK, TOCK!

8. Lewis T. Duck wakes up. "I don't want us to be late," he says, and he turns the clock back, too!

9. One by one, the others get up to turn the clock back: first Charlie, then Edward ...

10. Even Trader turns back the clock. TICK, TOCK! goes the clock, TICK, TOCK!

11. At last, everyone is asleep again, and Edward starts to snore quietly. But not for long ...

12. Brrrrrrrrrring! goes the big alarm clock. Brrrring, brrrrring, BRRRRRRRRRING!

13. The alarm clock wakes Charlie and the others. They jump up and bump into each other in the dark.

14. "Time to get up!" says Charlie. "Come on, you lot, or Captain Mildred will go without us."

15. But it's still night-time, and Captain Mildred is in bed. "She's fast asleep!" says Charlie.

16. Not for long! Charlie rings the big ship's bell as loudly as he can. "Wakey, wakey, Captain Mildred!"

 **BRITAINS**

Postman Pat™
Competition Time!

We've got some beautiful Postman Pat soft toys courtesy of Golden Bear and Britain's Petite Ltd, whose carefully created products are of the very highest standards. These lovely toys are authentic in every detail!

First Prize
Singing Postman Pat with Jess the Cat (35cm)
Simply squeeze Pat's tummy to hear him sing his song

Second Prize
Postman Pat Post Office
Includes telephone • ink pad and ink • stamps • parcels • play food • play money • postcards • postage stamps • colouring book • pension book • notebook • savings book • letterhead paper

Third Prize
Postman Pat and Jess soft toy (26cm)

plus 30 runners-up prizes of a Postman Pat beanie toy, Pull 'n' Go Van and wind-up Pat!

How to Enter:
All you have to do is answer this simple question:
"What is the name of the famous village where Pat lives and works?"

Write your answer on a postcard or the back of a sealed envelope (don't forget to include your name, address and age) and post to: Postman Pat Competition, Egmont World Limited, Deanway Technology Centre, Wilmslow Road, Handforth, Cheshire SK9 3FB.
(Closing date for entries is 26th January, 2001)

Rules
1. 33 winners will be chosen at random and notified by post.
2. Judges' decision will be final. No correspondence will be entered into.
3. The winners' names will be made available from Egmont World Ltd (on request) after 5th February 2001. Please enclose a stamped addressed envelope.
4. Employees (and their relatives) of Egmont World Ltd and their associated companies are not eligible to enter.
5. Entries are limited to one per person.
6. Competition is open to residents of the UK, Channel Islands and Ireland only.
7. The publishers reserve the right to vary prizes, subject to availability.
8. Closing date for entries is 26th January, 2001.

GOLDEN BEAR